Walt Disney's PINOCCHIO

Walt Disney's
PINOCCHIO

ADAPTED FROM THE FILM BY
GINA INGOGLIA
ILLUSTRATED BY
GIL DiCICCO

Disney
PRESS
NEW YORK

FIRST EDITION
1 3 5 7 9 10 8 6 4 2

Library of Congress Catalog Card Number: 91-73814
ISBN 1-56282-136-9/1-56282-137-7 (lib. ed.)

CHAPTER ONE

'll bet a lot of you folks out there don't believe in wishing on stars. You know—make a wish on the first star you see at night and your wish will come true? Well, I didn't believe in it either, and I thought I knew a lot! I'm pretty well traveled, you see. That's because I'm a cricket. The name's Jiminy. Jiminy Cricket. And you know how crickets get around— by hopping from hearth to hearth, visiting people's houses one after another. We get to see quite a bit of the world that way. And to me, this star-wishing business seemed like a lot of nonsense. But let me tell you what changed my mind.

It happened a long time ago. One chilly night my travels took me to a little village in the mountains. The stars were shining like diamonds, twinkling high above the tiled rooftops. That sleepy old town was as pretty as a picture!

I wandered along the dark streets, looking for a warm place to stay. Crickets travel light, and I was wearing all the clothes I owned. The only other possession I carried was my umbrella, in case of rain. I was shivering because my coat was pretty thin and my hat didn't do much good. My shoes were in bad shape, too—more of my toes were *out* than *in*!

At the foot of a crooked street I saw a light shining in a window. I hopped over and peeked in.

From what I could see, the place looked nice and cozy, with a fire crackling in the fireplace. Except for a little goldfish swimming in a glass bowl on a table, it looked as if no one was there. It seemed a shame for that fire to go to waste, so I went around to the front door, found a space I could squeeze under, and crawled in.

Being in a strange place, I didn't know what to expect, so I tiptoed

around for a quick look. Crickets can't be too careful, you know. Some people just don't welcome us into their homes. As soon as I was sure there was no one about, I scooted over to the fireplace.

As I stood warming myself with my back to the fire, I got a view of the whole place. And you never saw such a place! Hanging on the walls were dozens of ticking clocks—every kind imaginable—all carved out of wood. There were wooden music boxes, too, each one a work of art. And shelf after shelf of wonderful wooden toys!

It turned out that I was in a little shop owned by a wood-carver named Geppetto. His bed stood at one end of the room and his work-shop was set up at the other. Woodworking tools, pieces of wood, and paintbrushes lay ready to use on a worn workbench. Wood shavings were scattered on the floor.

One toy in particular caught my eye. It was a puppet sitting on the workbench. You know, one of those marionette things you work with strings? I took a closer look. It was a little boy puppet carved out of wood and dressed in a shirt and short pants. His hat had a red feather stuck in it. Even though his face wasn't all painted yet, I could tell the little guy was kind of cute. Good piece of wood, too! Just then I heard someone coming down the stairs, so I quickly hid behind one of the music boxes.

It was Geppetto! A black-and-white kitten followed close to his

heels. The old wood-carver headed straight for the workbench. After he polished his glasses on his apron, Geppetto peered closely at the puppet.

"It won't take much longer, Figaro," he said to the cat. "Just a little more paint and he's all finished!"

Geppetto picked up a small brush and stirred it in a jar of black paint. He carefully drew eyebrows on the puppet. As he worked, he hummed a happy little tune. Then he cleaned the brush, dipped it in red paint, and with one smooth stroke, he put a wide, rosy smile on the little wooden boy.

"See!" said Geppetto, setting down the brush. "That makes a big difference!"

He looked closely at the puppet and smiled. "I have just the name for you," he said. "It's Pinocchio!"

Geppetto crossed the room, turned on a couple of music boxes, and danced back to the workbench. He picked the puppet up by its strings and Pinocchio rose stiffly to his feet.

"Come on now, little woodenhead," Geppetto said and laughed, making the puppet walk. "We'll try you out—let's dance!"

The old man hummed and sang as he and Pinocchio danced around the workshop. Figaro pranced behind them, stepping lightly and waving his tail.

"Look, Figaro," said Geppetto. "How graceful my little wooden boy is!" He danced over to the goldfish bowl. "Let's introduce Pinocchio to Cleo."

Cleo swam over to look at Pinocchio. The pretty fish swirled around and around the bowl, blowing a trail of tiny bubbles.

"See, Pinocchio," said Geppetto, "my Cleo likes you!"

All at once, the clocks began to strike, filling the air with gongs, bells, cuckoos, and chimes. You never heard such a racket!

"It's getting late. Time for bed, my little fellow," said Geppetto. He carried Pinocchio back to the workbench and gently sat him down. "Look at him, Figaro," said the old man. "How real my Pinocchio looks. He almost looks alive. Wouldn't it be nice if he were a real boy!"

Then Geppetto sighed. "Oh well," he said and slowly walked across the room to his bed. "Come on, Figaro, let's get some sleep."

By this time, I was exhausted and found myself a comfortable violin in which to spend the night. I folded my coat under my head, settled down, and closed my eyes. "Look, Figaro!" I heard Geppetto say. "The wishing star!"

I turned to look, and there was Geppetto gazing out the window and wishing on a star!

"Star light, star bright," he said. "First star I see tonight, I wish I may, I wish I might, have the wish I make tonight!"

Then Geppetto said to Figaro, "You know what I wished? I wished that my little Pinocchio might become a *real* boy! Just think . . ."

"A very nice thought," I said, yawning. "But not at all practical!"

couldn't sleep. It was all those darn clocks—tick, tock, tockety, tickety, tick, tock! As I was lying there with my eyes wide open, staring into space, I became aware of something strange. The room was growing brighter!

The light seemed to be coming from outside, so I hopped onto the windowsill and looked out. One star, brighter than all the rest, glowed in the black night sky. Right before my eyes, it grew larger and larger. I could hardly believe it—the star was heading my way!

It floated in through the open window and settled down all a-twinkle right in the middle of the shop! I don't mind telling you, at first I was pretty scared. I mean, you don't see a sight like that every day! I frantically looked for a place to hide, and scrambled inside one of Geppetto's pipes. It was a pretty stuffy hiding place, but at least I was out of sight. Taking care not to be seen, I peeked out to see what would happen next.

In a moment or two, the dazzling starlight faded, but in its place there appeared a beautiful lady with golden hair! She held a wand in one hand and wore a long blue dress that sparkled like thousands of tiny stars. When she turned her back to me, I saw that she had *wings*! They were clear and shiny, like a spider's web covered with

morning dew. I shivered with excitement. As I live and breathe—I was looking at a real live fairy!

Our lovely visitor, who I later learned was the Blue Fairy, looked at Geppetto snoring softly in his sleep.

"Good Geppetto," she said. "You have given so much happiness to others, you deserve to have your wish come true."

The Blue Fairy looked around the room and saw Pinocchio sitting on the workbench, just as Geppetto had left him. Smiling, she went over to the little wooden puppet and touched him softly with her wand. As she did this, a bright light shimmered around Pinocchio.

"Little puppet made of pine," said the Blue Fairy. "Wake! The gift of life is thine!"

As soon as those magic words were spoken, Pinocchio opened his eyes! And I don't mean anyone pulled his strings. In fact, he didn't even have strings anymore. He moved all by himself. Pinocchio was *alive*! What they can't do these days!

Pinocchio lifted his hands and rubbed his eyes.

"I can move!" he said, looking at his hands. Then he covered his mouth.

"I can talk!" he said, and laughed out loud.

Pinocchio got onto his knees and, after a bit of a struggle, managed to stand.

"Look!" he shouted, tottering back and forth on the workbench, "I can walk, too!" He toppled backward and sat down with a thump.

"Yes, Pinocchio," said the Blue Fairy, trying not to laugh. "I have given you life."

"Why?" asked Pinocchio.

"Because tonight," she explained to him, "Geppetto wished for a real boy!"

Pinocchio thought this over for a minute and then pointed to himself.

"Am I a *real* boy?" he asked.

The Blue Fairy smiled and patted his wooden head.

"No, Pinocchio," she said. "Making Geppetto's wish come true will be entirely up to you."

"Up to *me*?" asked Pinocchio in a tiny voice. "How?"

"First you must prove that you are brave, truthful, and unselfish," said the Blue Fairy. "Then, someday, you will be a real boy!"

Pinocchio clapped his hands.

"A real boy!" he shouted. "I can't wait!"

"You must learn to choose between right and wrong," continued the Blue Fairy.

Pinocchio was puzzled. "Right and wrong?" he asked. "How will I know which is which?"

"Your conscience will tell you," she explained.

"Oh good," said Pinocchio, looking relieved. "What's a conscience?"

I was so caught up with this whole thing that I popped out of my hiding place and spoke right up.

"I'll tell you, Pinocchio!" I explained as I climbed out of the pipe. "A conscience is that small voice inside people that they never listen to. That's the trouble with the world today . . ."

I paused to catch my breath and continued, "You see . . ."

Pinocchio looked at me in wide-eyed amazement.

"Are *you* my conscience?" he asked.

"Who, me?" I said, suddenly feeling foolish.

The Blue Fairy leaned over and asked me a question that would change my whole life.

"Would you like to be Pinocchio's conscience?" she asked.

"Well, uh, well, uh," I said. I felt flattered and my face grew all hot and red. "Sure!" I managed to say at last.

"Very well. What is your name?" she asked, and smiled.

Now *that* was something I could answer right away! I pulled off my hat and bowed low.

"Cricket's the name," I said, politely. "Jiminy Cricket."

"Well, how do you do, Jiminy," she said. "I am the Blue Fairy."

Then she asked me to kneel. I wondered what was going on, but I did as I was instructed. The Blue Fairy tapped me on each shoulder with her wand, and as soon as the wand touched me, I was surrounded by a shimmering light. I remembered what had happened to Pinocchio and I wondered what was going to happen to *me*!

"I dub you Pinocchio's conscience," said the Blue Fairy. "You are Lord High Keeper of the Knowledge of Right and Wrong. You will be Pinocchio's counselor in moments of temptation and his guide along the straight and narrow path."

I was impressed. Was I really all those things she said?

"Arise, Sir Jiminy Cricket!" she said.

Sir Jiminy Cricket! Now I knew I must be dreaming!

When I got to my feet, I realized all my clothes were different.

The Blue Fairy had given me a brand-new outfit! I had a smart-looking hat, a jacket with no buttons missing, and a pair of shiny shoes without holes. I even had a snazzy-looking umbrella. I felt pretty special. Being a conscience wasn't so bad!

"My, my" was all I managed to say. "That's pretty swell. But, uh, don't I get a badge?" It occurred to me I might need something to make it all—you know—official.

"Well," said the Blue Fairy, smiling at me. "We'll see."

"If I ever do get a badge," I said, hoping I didn't sound too greedy, "could you please make it a gold one?"

"Maybe" was all the Blue Fairy would say. Then she turned to Pinocchio. "Be a good boy," she said. "And remember, always let your conscience be your guide."

She meant me! I can't tell you how good I felt. The Blue Fairy waved good-bye to us and faded away.

Pinocchio waved back. "Good-bye," he called. "And thanks for everything!"

ow that Pinocchio and I were alone, I decided I ought to give the little guy a bit of advice. After all, it *was* my job!

"Pinocchio, my boy," I said, trying to sound important but not too bossy, "sit down. Maybe you and I better have a little heart-to-heart talk."

Pinocchio flopped down in front of me. "Why?" he asked.

"Well, you want to be a real boy, don't you?" I said.

"Uh-huh!" said Pinocchio.

"Then you'd better listen to what I have to say." I cleared my throat and went on. "The world is full of temptations. . . ."

"Temptations?" asked Pinocchio.

"Yes," I said. "Temptations. They're the wrong things that seem right at the time. But, uh, even though the right things may seem wrong sometimes, sometimes the wrong things may be right at the wrong time, and sometimes it's the other way around. Do you understand, Pinocchio?"

"Nope," he said, shaking his head. "But I'm going to do *right*!"

"Good!" I said. "And I'm going to help you."

As Pinocchio struggled to his feet, I thought of something important I'd left out. "If we ever get separated and you need me," I said, "just whistle and I'll come as fast as I can."

"That's a good idea!" said Pinocchio. "What's 'whistle'?"

"It's not hard," I said. "You just pucker up your lips and blow."

I proceeded to whistle a little tune for him. I'm a skilled whistler, if I do say so myself. When I'd finished my demonstration, I asked Pinocchio to give it a try.

Pinocchio closed his eyes, puckered his lips, and held his breath. His face got redder and redder until I thought he might burst.

"Blow, for heaven's sake!" I instructed. *"Blow!"*

Pinocchio blew, all right—he practically blew me right off my feet!

"Not so hard, Pinocchio," I said, feeling rattled. "Do it gently— like this."

I whistled a short airy tune while Pinocchio watched carefully. When I was through, he closed his eyes and puckered up his lips once again. I stepped out of the way. Much to my amazement—he whistled!

"You've got it, Pinoke!" I shouted. "You can whistle!"

"Let's whistle together!" shouted Pinocchio, all pleased and proud.

He got to his feet and started strutting across the shelf, whistling happily. We were in the middle of our sixth song when Pinocchio got his foot caught in a pot of paint. He stumbled off the shelf with a *crash*! Luckily he wasn't hurt at all, but the loud noise had awakened Geppetto. "Who's there?" he called from his bed.

Geppetto climbed out of bed and, with Figaro right behind him, looked nervously about the room.

"What's going on?" he asked. "Is anybody in there?"

"It's me!" Pinocchio cried out excitedly. "Here I am!"

Geppetto peered through his eyeglasses and saw Pinocchio standing in the middle of the floor.

"Pinocchio?" he asked. "How did you get over there?" He shuffled across the shop and picked him up.

"I walked here," Pinocchio said proudly.

"Oh, you did," said Geppetto, straightening the feather on Pinocchio's hat. Then he jumped in surprise. "Oh—you're *talking*!" he gasped.

"Uh-huh," said Pinocchio. "I can whistle, too."

Geppetto shook his head in amazement. He took out his handkerchief, polished his glasses, and looked closely at Pinocchio.

"I'm—I'm dreaming," he stammered. "That must be it. I'm still asleep."

"You're not dreaming, Father," said Pinocchio. "The Blue Fairy came. . . ."

"The Blue Fairy?" said Geppetto.

"Uh-huh," said Pinocchio. "She was beautiful. She had a sparkling wand and everything. And I got my own conscience!"

"A conscience?" said Geppetto. He looked a little dazed and confused.

"And someday," added Pinocchio, pointing to himself, "I won't be made out of wood. I'm going to be a real boy!"

"You're alive!" he said. Geppetto picked up Pinocchio and kissed him. "It's my wish—it's come true, Figaro!" he said, laughing and crying at the same time.

"Just look at you!" he said joyfully, holding Pinocchio in the air. "My own boy!"

Figaro peeked at Pinocchio from behind Geppetto's legs.

"Look, my Pinocchio is alive!" Geppetto said to his pet. "Pinocchio, say hello to Figaro."

"Hello to Figaro," echoed Pinocchio, petting the shy little kitten.

"Oh, I almost forgot!" said Geppetto. He picked up Pinocchio and carried him over to Cleo's bowl. "Look, Cleo," he said. "Meet Pinocchio!"

Pinocchio looked closely at Cleo and Cleo looked back at Pinocchio.

"She's my little water baby," said Geppetto. "Isn't she cute?"

"Yes, cute," said Pinocchio, sticking his finger into the water. Cleo waved her tail at Pinocchio and swam merrily around the bowl. Then she jumped into the air, gave Pinocchio a watery kiss on his nose, and fell back into the bowl with a splash. Laughing out loud, Geppetto picked up his accordion and began to play.

"This calls for a celebration!" he cried.

Geppetto wound up several of the music boxes. It was the second time that night I'd watched Geppetto dance with Pinocchio. But this time it was different. Now Geppetto wasn't pulling any strings to make his little wooden boy move; Pinocchio was dancing all by himself! The old wood-carver sang happily as he waltzed with his new son. It was a wonderful party!

After a while, Geppetto stopped dancing and looked at his pocket watch.

"Maybe we'd better go to bed," he said, puffing a bit.

"Why?" asked Pinocchio.

"Everybody has to sleep," Geppetto explained to his little boy. "Figaro goes to sleep—and Cleo, too. And besides, tomorrow you've got to go to school."

"I do?" said Pinocchio. "Why?"

"To learn things," said Geppetto. "And to get smart!"

Geppetto carried Pinocchio to bed and tucked him in for the night.

"Good night, my dear son," he said. "Sweet dreams."

"Sweet dreams to you, Father," said Pinocchio.

I was pretty tired myself, and I had a big day ahead of me. In the morning I had to go to school with Pinocchio and keep him out of trouble.

I found an empty, cozy-looking matchbox lying on the warm hearth. It made a perfect bed! I climbed into the box and, taking special care, folded my handsome new coat, put it under my head, and pulled the matchbox cover up to my chin.

What a night it had been! The events of the past hours floated pleasantly through my head, and in a few minutes, I was sound asleep. And, most regrettably, I overslept!

he next morning I woke up with the sun shining in my eyes. Squinting, I peered up at an old cuckoo clock on the wall. Geppetto had sent Pinocchio to school hours ago! What a fine conscience I turned out to be—late the first day! Oh well, I thought, the little guy can't get into much trouble between here and school. Boy, was I ever wrong!

*   *   *

As Pinocchio walked through the village to the schoolhouse, two other characters were fated to cross his path. Honest John—who was anything but honest—and his companion, Gideon.

"Ah, Gideon," Honest John said to his sidekick as they watched the village children making their way to school that morning. "Thirsty minds rushing to the fountain of knowledge. School," he continued, "such a noble institution."

Then they stopped in front of a colorful poster pasted on a brick wall. It read:

The Great
STROMBOLI
· MARIONETTE SHOW ·

"So," said Honest John, "that old rascal Stromboli's back in town, ha, ha. Remember, Giddy, the time I tied strings on you and tried to pass you off as a puppet!"

Gideon nodded shyly, but Honest John burst into laughter. He was laughing so hard, he hardly noticed when Pinocchio skipped by.

"A little wooden boy, ha, ha," he said.

And then he turned.

"*A wooden boy!*" he said in a startled voice. "Look, Giddy! A live puppet without strings. A thing like that must be worth a fortune to someone. But who?" He stroked his chin and thought hard.

"That's it!" he shouted, looking up. "Stromboli!" And with that, he and Gideon ran off to find Pinocchio.

Minutes later, Pinocchio came skipping around a corner, and with a thump, he fell to the ground. Honest John had tripped him with his cane.

"Oh, how clumsy of me!" Honest John said, pulling Pinocchio to his feet.

"I'm all right," said Pinocchio, smiling. He bent down and gathered his schoolbooks from the ground. "I'm on my way to school," he said proudly.

"I see," said Honest John. "Then you haven't heard of the easy road to success. I'm speaking of the theater, my boy. You know, bright lights, music—and *fame*!"

"Fame?" asked Pinocchio.

"Why, yes," continued Honest John, "and with your face, your personality, your physique . . . why, you're a natural-born actor!"

"I am?" said Pinocchio.

"You belong in the theater," urged Honest John.

"But I'm going . . ."

"Straight to the top!" Honest John finished Pinocchio's sentence. Then the three marched off happily, singing a song about the gay life of an actor.

Before long, Pinocchio had forgotten all about school and was singing his way to the theater.

*   *   *

Meanwhile, I hurried along the winding streets, hunting for the village schoolhouse. I was about to ask directions when I heard the sound of marching feet and singing voices. I looked behind me to see who it was.

Two unusual-looking characters were parading down the sidewalk. Although I didn't know it then, it was Honest John and Gideon. Both wore top hats and carried canes. Their worn-out coats, fancy when new, were now ragged and patched. And there was Pinocchio, marching right between them, singing at the top of his lungs.

"Hey, Pinoke!" I yelled, and tried to block their way. "Where're you going?"

They didn't see me and nearly ran over me.

"Wait! Halt!" I shouted, pursuing them. They were getting far ahead of me. I could hear Pinocchio's voice loud and clear, singing that song about show business. Show business! What did Pinocchio know about show business!

I never ran and hopped so fast. Using my last bit of strength, I caught up to Honest John and grabbed on to his tail. I don't know how I ever did it—I managed to make my way up his back and then to the top of his head.

"Hey, Pinoke!" I shouted, clutching Honest John's tattered hat. "Look up here!"

No luck. Nobody heard me. Then I had an idea. I took a deep breath and whistled. It was the loudest I'd whistled in my life—I didn't even know I had it in me. And it did the trick! The three of them came to a sudden halt.

"What was *that*?" asked Honest John, as he shook his head and rubbed his ear.

"Oh, it's Jiminy!" said Pinocchio, looking up at me. "Hello! What are you doing up there?"

Not wanting to be caught, I popped open my sturdy umbrella and parachuted to the ground. Quickly, I hid among some wildflowers blooming by the side of the road. While Honest John and Gideon examined the hat, I tried to get Pinocchio's attention.

"Psst! Pinoke!" I whispered. "Over here!"

Pinocchio ran over. The little fellow seemed delighted to see me.

"Oh, Jiminy," said Pinocchio. "I'm going to be an actor!"

Now this was definitely a job for a conscience!

"All right, son," I said. "Take it easy now. Remember what I said about temptation?"

"Uh-huh," said Pinocchio.

"Well," I said, pointing to Honest John, who was still occupied with his hat, "that's *it*!"

"Oh, no, Jiminy," said Pinocchio. "That's Mr. Honest John with his friend Gideon! They stopped me on my way to school. They have a job for me in show business. There will be music, applause, and *fame*! My name will be up in lights—six feet high! I'm going straight to the top. You and Father will be proud of me, Jiminy—you'll see!"

Without even meeting Honest John and Gideon, I didn't like them. I've always thought myself a good judge of character, and I could tell these two characters weren't right for Pinocchio. I had to work fast.

"You can't go into show business," I told him. "Here's what I want you to tell them. Say thank you just the same—you're sorry, but you've got to go to school."

"Uh-huh," said Pinocchio.

Good! I thought. What a relief. I'd gotten through to him.

Honest John shook his hat a few more times. Still finding nothing in it, he brushed it off and put it back on his head. Then he and Gideon headed our way.

"Pinocchio, my boy!" called Honest John. "Time to go!"

"Now you tell them what I said," I urged the little guy.

"Pinocchio, oh, Pinocchio!" Honest John sang out again. "Ah, there you are! Let's go! On to the theater!"

"Good-bye, Jiminy," said Pinocchio, waving to me. "Good-bye!"

Good-bye! What did he mean, *good-bye*!

Somewhat in a state of shock, I watched as Honest John and Gideon skipped off arm in arm with Pinocchio.

"Hey, Pinoke!" I shouted in vain. "Wait! You can't go. . . ."

But he didn't wait; he went. I had failed. What would I tell Geppetto?

I decided not to tell him anything. I'd go after Pinocchio myself. That was to be my first big mistake!

CHAPTER FIVE

y the time I'd decided to go after them, Honest John and Gideon had disappeared with Pinocchio. Desperate, I ran down the winding streets, not knowing where to look. Where had they gone? It didn't take me too long to find out.

There was a puppet show being held at the edge of town. A noisy crowd had gathered in front of the outdoor stage. Pretty soon there wasn't an empty seat in the place. I hopped up to a good spot on a lamppost and waited for the show to begin.

A fat man strutted out in front of the stage. He had a shiny bald head, a curly black mustache, and a long beard. A wide red sash was stretched tight around his enormous belly. He held up his pudgy hands and waited for the crowd to settle down. Then he cleared his throat and spoke.

"Ladieees and gentlemen," he announced loudly. "I am Stromboli, the master showman. By special permission of the management—that's also me—I present to you an act you will absoloootely refuse to believe!"

Just as I had disliked Honest John and Gideon at first sight, I disliked Stromboli, too. I was afraid Pinocchio had gotten involved

with very bad company indeed, and I felt disgusted with this whole affair.

"I introdoooce to you," Stromboli boasted enthusiastically, "the only marionette who can sing and dance—absoloootely without the aid of strings! The one and only—Peeenocchio!"

A few trumpets blared and the curtain rose. A spotlight lit a small figure in the center of the stage. Sure enough, it was Pinocchio. He stood poised at the top of a short set of steps.

"Go ahead, Pinocchio," I mumbled. "Make a fool out of yourself. Then maybe you'll listen to your conscience!"

When the band began to play, Pinocchio started down the steps, singing. He'd hardly begun when he tripped over his feet, flipped down the steps, and landed flat on his face.

Stromboli was furious! He ran to the stage, grabbed Pinocchio, and started to yell. But when he heard the crowd laughing at Pinocchio's fall, he suddenly smiled widely.

"Heh, heh, cute kid!" he said, patting Pinocchio on the head and setting him back on his feet.

Pinocchio went on with his act. He sang a song about not needing any strings to move. Then he performed several other numbers with

a dozen or so dancing marionettes. He got tangled up in their strings a few times, but on the whole, he did very well. When the show was over, the audience went wild and threw coins and flowers at Pinocchio. They loved him! Stromboli bowed happily next to Pinocchio, patting him on the head a few times.

Gosh, maybe I was wrong. Little Pinoke was a hit! Maybe show business *was* the life for him!

While Pinocchio bowed and waved back at the whistling, cheering crowd, I turned and walked away. I guessed he wouldn't be needing me anymore.

It started to rain and I put up my umbrella. I'd have to find a dry place to spend the night.

As I hopped over puddles and sloshed along, I wondered what

Pinocchio was doing. Was the little guy safe and dry? Of course he was, I told myself. Stromboli wouldn't let anything happen to Pinocchio. With Pinocchio, Stromboli's show would become world famous. I had to admit it—show business might be a glamorous life after all.

But what would happen to Geppetto? How happy would *he* be? Wouldn't he be lonesome without the little fellow? I didn't know it then, but Geppetto was worried sick. He was frantically searching for his son, out in the pouring rain.

*　　*　　*

Inside Stromboli's traveling wagon, Pinocchio sat on a table, watching the puppet master count the evening's earnings. Stromboli was spearing olives and all sorts of other delicacies with a large knife—

the same knife he was using to slide stacks of shiny coins from one side of the table to the other.

"Bravo, Pinocchio," he said with his mouth full.

"You mean I'm good?" Pinocchio asked.

"You are sensational!" answered Stromboli, with a laugh.

"Does that mean I'm an actor?" Pinocchio asked eagerly.

"Sure," said Stromboli, never looking up from his money.

"I'll run right home and tell Father!" Pinocchio said.

This time, Stromboli looked up—in fact, he gulped his food and wheezed. "Going home?" he said in an angry voice. Then he waved his finger at Pinocchio and laughed. "Very funny, Pinocchio."

Pinocchio laughed, too.

Then Stromboli picked Pinocchio up and, still laughing, staggered around the wagon, causing all the puppets hanging on the wall to shake. He stopped suddenly by a hanging birdcage and quickly threw

Pinocchio in. Then he locked the cage with a giant padlock.

"*This* will be your home—where I can always find you!" he yelled in a loud and frightening voice.

"No! No! No!" Pinocchio yelled, tears swelling in his eyes.

"Yes! Yes! Yes!" answered Stromboli. "You will make lots of money for me, and when you are too old—I will chop you into fire-wood!"

"Let me out of here!" Pinocchio screamed, frantically shaking the bars of his cage.

"Good night, my little wooden gold mine!" said Stromboli. Then he turned and left Pinocchio alone in the back of the wagon.

Pinocchio struggled and shook the bars of the cage until he was thrown back by the sudden movement of the wagon.

He whistled as hard as he could for Jiminy. Then he cried in despair, "Jiminy! Oh, Jiminy, where are you?"

didn't know it, but the poor little guy was calling for *me*! With all the thunder and rain, I couldn't hear him! Gusty winds, lifting me right off my feet, pushed me along the wet, skiddy streets. Lightning flashed all around me. My umbrella was no help, and soon I was soaked. My new clothes were wringing wet and my shoes had lost their shine.

Then a large rickety wagon creaked past me, pulled by a worn-out old horse. The driver was singing loudly and I recognized his voice immediately—it was Stromboli! There goes Pinocchio, off to a life of fame and fortune. The world at his feet, I thought. I just hoped he'd be happy.

As I watched the wagon rumble over the cobblestones, I had a sudden yearning to wish Pinocchio good luck. I wanted to say good-bye once more before he disappeared from my life forever. Sure, why not? So I dashed down the slippery street, caught up with Stromboli's wagon, and pulled myself up and into the back.

"Pinocchio!" I said, peering inside the dimly lit wagon. "It's me— your old friend, Jiminy. Are you in here?"

"Jiminy! Gee, I'm glad to see you!" I heard Pinocchio answer.

My eyes adjusted to the gloom and I was able to see better.

Marionettes hung everywhere and others lay where they'd been tossed in a heap on the wagon floor.

Then I saw Pinocchio—looking at me through bars. He was locked up in a big wooden birdcage!

"Pinocchio! What's happened to you?" I cried, running over to him.

"Mr. Stromboli put me in here. This cage is going to be my home, where he can find me—*always*!" sobbed my little friend. "Mr. Stromboli said I'm going to make lots of money for him. And he won't let me see my father—*ever again*!"

Pinocchio paused to catch his breath and a tear trickled down his cheek.

"And Jiminy," he added, wide-eyed, "Mr. Stromboli said he's going to take me all over the world—to Paris and London—and Constantinople! And when I'm old and worn, he's going to chop me into firewood!"

I was furious.

"Oh—is that so!" I said, taking a look at the padlock on the cage door.

"Uh-huh," nodded Pinocchio, his eyes shiny with tears.

"Don't you worry, son. I'll have you out of this cage in a jiffy!"

"You will?" asked Pinocchio, brightening up a bit.

"Why, sure," I said. "You didn't know I was an expert locksmith, did you? Well, I am!"

Because of my size and technical know-how, I could fit inside any lock and open it in a matter of seconds.

I climbed into the lock to have a look around. Uh-oh. It wasn't going to be as easy as I thought. The insides of this old lock were dusty and caked with rust. I poked and pried and tugged, but the lock didn't budge. It was impossible to open it without a key.

"Uh . . . needs a little oil," I said. I tried again but it was no use.

"Can't you undo it?" Pinocchio asked, listening to my grunts and grumbles.

"Nope. Must be one of the old models," I replied, both depressed at my failure and worried about Pinocchio's predicament. Things looked pretty hopeless. It would take a miracle to get him out!

"Gee, Jiminy," said Pinocchio, sinking to his knees and sitting on the grimy cage floor. "I should have listened to you."

"No," I said, accepting the blame. "I should have kept my eye on you." I squeezed between the bars and rested against Pinocchio's knee.

"I guess I'll never see Father again," he sobbed, and one of his tears dropped onto my hat.

"Take it easy, son," I said. "I'll think of something." But I hadn't the faintest idea *what*.

I noticed the rain had stopped and I looked out at the stars appearing in the sky. Glittering brightly, one star suddenly grew larger and began spinning toward Stromboli's wagon.

"Pinocchio!" I gasped, getting to my feet. "It's that star again! I think the Blue Fairy's headed our way!"

"Oh, Jiminy! What'll I tell her?" asked Pinocchio. "She wanted me to be a good boy and to learn right from wrong."

"You might tell her the truth," I suggested.

I had no sooner gotten the words out of my mouth than the wagon was filled with whirling, twinkling starlight. As before, it vanished, and the Blue Fairy appeared in its place. Pinocchio took one look at her and hid his face in his hands. I felt pretty embarrassed myself. What a conscience *I'd* turned out to be!

The Blue Fairy walked over to the cage.

"Why, Pinocchio!" she said in her gentle voice.

"Uh—er—hello," stammered Pinocchio.

Then she spotted me.

"Sir Jiminy!" she said.

"Well—uh—this *is* a pleasant surprise," I said, sounding foolish and taking off my hat.

"Pinocchio, why didn't you go to school?" the Blue Fairy asked.

Oh, brother, I thought. This is it!

"Well, you see," explained Pinocchio. "I was going to school until I met somebody. . . ."

I was proud of the little guy—he was going to tell her the truth!

"Met somebody?" asked the Blue Fairy.

"Right," said Pinocchio. "Two big monsters—with big green eyes!"

My heart sank.

"Monsters?" asked the Blue Fairy. "Weren't you afraid?"

"No ma'am," said Pinocchio. "But they tied me in a big sack!"

"You don't say . . . ," said the beautiful fairy.

I was shocked. Pinocchio continued to tell one lie after another. But, even more shocking, with each lie, Pinocchio's wooden nose grew longer and longer! By the time he'd finished, his nose stuck out through the bars of the cage. Not only that, the tip of his nose had sprouted leaves—complete with a bird's nest and a chirping family of birds!

"Oh! Oh! Look! My nose!" cried Pinocchio. "What's happening to it?"

"Perhaps you haven't been telling the truth, Pinocchio," said the Blue Fairy.

"Perhaps!" I chimed in.

"You see, Pinocchio," added the Blue Fairy, "a lie keeps growing and growing until it's as plain as the nose on your face."

"I'll never lie again," promised Pinocchio, watching a bird flutter around his head. "Honest I won't!"

"Please, Your Honor—I mean Miss Fairy—give him another chance," I begged. "And I'll try to do my job better, too!"

The Blue Fairy looked us up and down.

"I'll forgive you this once, Pinocchio," she said. "But this is the last time I can help you. Remember, a boy who won't be good might just as well be made of wood!"

The Blue Fairy touched Pinocchio's nose with her magic wand and, in a dazzle of light, she vanished.

"Look, Jiminy! My old nose is back!" said Pinocchio, happily tapping it with his fingers.

To my great delight, I saw that the cage was unlocked.

"You're free!" I cried. "Come on, Pinoke!"

The two of us scrambled to the back of the wagon and jumped out. We ran to the side of the road and watched Stromboli and his wagon disappear around the bend.

"Toodle-oo, Stromboli," I said.

"Good-bye, Mr. Stromboli," Pinocchio called.

The wicked man was still singing—he'd never heard a thing!

I looked at my watch and saw it was already close to midnight.

"Let's get out of here," I said to Pinocchio, "before anything else happens!"

And as we headed back to town, I made my second big mistake.

"Come on, slowpoke," I said to Pinocchio. "I'll race you home!"

CHAPTER SEVEN

I n a dark tavern not very far from where the race began, Honest John was, once again, up to no good.

He sat at a table with Gideon and an evil-looking coachman. All three were drinking beer and talking in low voices.

"Now, coachman," Honest John was saying, "what's your proposition?"

"Well," said the coachman, puffing his pipe and looking around the room suspiciously, "I'm collecting little boys—you know, the bad ones that play 'ooky from school."

"Ahhh!" said Honest John with a knowing nod, even though he didn't really know.

"And I takes them to Pleasure Island," continued the coachman.

"Pleasure Island!" the two sly characters said together.

The three huddled over the table as the coachman continued. "There's no risk. They never come back—as boys!"

"Ohhh!" said Honest John and Gideon.

Then the coachman leaned even closer. "I've got a coachload leaving at midnight. Any good prospects you find—bring them to me and you'll be paid well. I've got plenty of gold. . . ."

"Yes, yes," answered Honest John, chuckling. "Yes." And they got up to leave.

No sooner had Honest John and Gideon left the tavern than Pinocchio came running by.

"Well, well," said Honest John, blocking Pinocchio's way. "What's your rush?"

"I've got to beat Jiminy home," said Pinocchio, his arms and legs still in motion.

"But what about acting?" Honest John asked.

"I don't want to be an actor anymore," said Pinocchio. "Stromboli was mean, and I learned my lesson."

"My poor boy!" cried Honest John, clasping Pinocchio's face in his hands. "You must be a nervous wreck!" He turned Pinocchio's head right, then left.

"It's just as I thought," he continued. "You have a compound of transmission of the pandemonium with percussion of spasmodic frantic

disintegration! There's only one cure—a vacation! On Pleasure Island!"

"Pleasure Island?" said Pinocchio. "But I can't go. I've got to . . ."

"Why, sure you can," said Honest John. "I'm giving you *my*
ticket!"

"Uh, thanks," said Pinocchio, "but I'm . . ."

"Tut-tut. I insist," interrupted Honest John. "Now come. The
coach departs at midnight."

*   *   *

When I reached the center of town, I got the shock of my life!
Instead of trying to beat me home, there was Pinocchio, walking arm
in arm with those two rascals, Honest John and Gideon.

"Pinocchio! Hey, Pinoke, come back!" I shouted.

But Pinocchio never turned around. He was heading out of town!

Fortunately I was able to keep up with them this time. Honest John was singing loudly as usual—only this time the song wasn't about show business. Now he was singing about some spot called Pleasure Island. Where and what was Pleasure Island? I wondered. Knowing Honest John, whatever Pleasure Island was, I was sure it wouldn't be anything like its name!

A stagecoach, pulled by a team of sleepy-looking donkeys, stood waiting at the main road out of town. It was filled to bursting with noisy little boys, all excited, laughing, and happy. How could all these boys be out in the middle of the night? I wondered.

A stocky, round-faced coachman sat in the driver's seat, holding

a long whip. Honest John handed Pinocchio over to him, and I found a place I could hang on to at the back of the coach. Pinocchio was seated next to a rough-looking boy with red hair. Every now and then the boy would take his slingshot and shoot at things along the road. I hoped he and Pinocchio wouldn't become friends. But no sooner had I hoped for this than the boy engaged Pinocchio in conversation.

"M'name's Lampwick," he said to Pinocchio. "They say Pleasure Island's a swell joint," he continued. "No school, no cops—you can tear da joint apart!"

At the stroke of midnight, the coachman cracked the whip, the coach lurched forward, and we were off.

Well, I thought, here we go again.

After a long and bouncy ride we reached the harbor. The boys boarded a large steamboat tied to the docks and before long we were at sea.

It was a beautiful night to be out on the water. As I looked up at the twinkling stars, I thought of the Blue Fairy. She said she wouldn't give Pinocchio any more help, and I hoped he wouldn't need it. But still, I felt a bit uneasy.

Pleasure Island loomed into sight. A gigantic wall of rock surrounded the entire island. Built into the wall were two enormous gates and a heavy wood-and-iron drawbridge. After the boat docked, the drawbridge slowly lowered and the gates creaked open.

I could hardly believe what I saw! Pleasure Island was an amusement park full of thrilling rides and all kinds of food that boys love!

Pushing and shoving, the boys scrambled out of the boat; then, yelling, they scattered in all directions. I tried to catch up with Pinocchio, but he was off and running with Lampwick, and I quickly lost sight of them.

Standing near the entrance, a man greeted the boys in a hearty voice and welcomed them to Pleasure Island.

"Hurry! Hurry! Hurry!" he loudly encouraged them. "Right here, boys! Get your cake, pie, and ice cream! Eat all you can! Be a pig! Stuff yourselves! It's all free, boys! It's all free! Hurry! Hurry! Hurry!"

The boys ran all over the place. They gobbled up fistfuls of gooey chocolate candies and stuffed themselves with hot apple pies, double-decker ice-cream cones, and fried chicken.

But these boys didn't just eat and go on the rides! They scribbled all over the walls, smoked cigars, and littered the ground with dozens

of empty bottles and candy wrappers. They broke windows with bricks and stones. But nobody ever told them to stop! In fact, the worse they behaved, the more they were encouraged to be bad! They were

urged to pick fights. There was even a brand-new, furnished house for the boys to destroy! I watched, stunned, as plants were tipped over, shutters were torn from their hinges—a group of boys even pushed a piano down the front steps! I was horrified!

I could tell these boys had been in trouble long before they came to Pleasure Island. They joked about skipping school and running away from home. This place was like heaven to them and they were enjoying every minute.

Desperate, I searched for Pinocchio. I knew this was no place for him. Hours dragged by and I still hadn't found him. By the time the sun was ready to come up, the fairgrounds were in ruins and all was quiet and deserted. Where had everybody gone? By now I was convinced there was definitely something evil about the place!

CHAPTER EIGHT

I was exhausted, but I continued to search for Pinocchio through the now-wrecked fairgrounds. I spotted a dim light in a nearby building and decided to investigate. Faint voices came from inside and I recognized one of them—it was Pinocchio's!

Following the sound, I walked into a dirty, smoke-filled room. There was Pinocchio, kneeling on a pool table, smoking a cigar! And with him was the redheaded boy, Lampwick. Just as I thought—I knew he'd be bad company for Pinocchio!

"Where do you suppose all the kids went, Lampy?" Pinocchio was asking.

"They're around here somewhere," said Lampwick. "Stop worryin'—you're having a good time, ain't ya?"

"I sure am!" said Pinocchio.

I couldn't stand to listen for another minute. "So *this* is where I find you!" I scolded Pinocchio. "How do you ever expect to be a *real* boy! Look at yourself—smoking a cigar! Playing pool! You're coming right home with me!" I ordered, grabbing Pinocchio by the arm.

But before I could say another word, that redheaded boy picked me up right off my feet!

"Who's the beetle?" Lampwick asked Pinocchio, dangling me by my coat collar.

"Hey, put me down," I yelled and kicked.

"He's my conscience," explained Pinocchio. "He tells me what's right and wrong."

"Oh, yeah?" said the bully. "You mean to tell me you take orders from a grasshopper?"

"Put me down this instant!" I demanded, and thank heavens he dropped me to my feet. I brushed off my coat and pulled myself together. Then I climbed up onto the pool table.

"It wouldn't hurt you to take orders from *your* conscience—if you have one!" I said indignantly. I sat on the eight ball, arms folded across my chest, and awaited Lampwick's response.

"Screwball in the corner pocket," was what he said, taking careful aim. Before I knew it, *I* was bounced into the corner pocket! I was nearly crushed by the six ball, but I jumped out of the way just in time. I pulled myself back up to the table and headed right for Lampwick.

"Why, you young hoodlum!" I called out, waving my fist.

"Don't be angry with Lampwick, Jiminy," said Pinocchio. "He's my best friend!"

His best friend!

"And what am I?" I asked, hurt and furious. *"Just your conscience?"*

"But Jiminy," said Pinocchio, "Lampwick says a guy only lives once!"

That was it! I was fed up! I didn't know what kind of a mess Pinocchio had gotten himself into, but I was clearly not wanted—so I walked away.

When I got outside, I headed back toward the entrance. Maybe I could find a way out of this miserable place! The gates were still shut, but luckily I discovered a crack big enough to crawl through.

I came upon an unexpected and strange sight. The dock was crowded with dozens of braying donkeys that were being stuffed into wooden crates and loaded onto the steamboat.

The coachman who had driven us here was yelling, "Come on, you blokes, keep 'em movin'!" Where had all these donkeys come from? Just then another batch of donkeys was led to the coachman.

"And what might be your name?" he asked one of the donkeys, who strangely enough was wearing a sailor's top.

"Alexander," the donkey replied.

"Take him back!" ordered the coachman. "He can still talk."

"Still talk!" I repeated out loud.

"Quiet! Stop that noise!" the coachman yelled, cracking his whip in the air. "You boys have had your fun—now pay for it!"

Boys? I suddenly realized what was going on and *who* was paying what price! All the bad boys had been turned into donkeys! They were being shipped off to hard jobs—pulling heavy loads and working in mines! And someone was going to make a fortune selling them all.

I had to get back to Pinocchio before he was turned into a donkey,

too! I ran back through the fairgrounds as fast as I could.

When I arrived, I heard loud braying and thumping sounds. I saw it was already too late for his friend Lampwick! The unfortunate creature was no longer a boy—he was a donkey! Carrying on something awful, Lampwick crashed around the room, kicking his hooves in the air, knocking over furniture, and braying pitifully.

Then I looked at Pinocchio. He looked at me with tears in his

eyes. He had already sprouted two droopy donkey ears and a long
brown tail!

"Pinocchio!" I screamed. "The boys—they're *all* donkeys like
Lampwick! Come on—quick! Maybe if we get away fast enough you
won't get any worse!"

We wasted no time. I led Pinocchio up to a high, rocky cliff that
I knew was our only way out. I kept looking back at Pinocchio to see
if he'd changed any more. But, fortunately, he was still the same—
except for those dreadful ears and that tail. We reached the top of

the cliff and peered over the edge. "You've got to jump!" I yelled to Pinocchio. We closed our eyes and leapt into the water below.

By the time we reached the shore, we were both exhausted.

"Are you all right?" I heard Pinocchio ask.

"I thought we'd never make it!" I sputtered, blinking my blurry eyes and shaking the water out of my ears. "But it certainly feels good to be back on land. Come on, Pinocchio, let's get home."

We ran all the way back to Geppetto's house.

CHAPTER NINE

inocchio could hardly wait to see his father.

"Father, Father, I'm home!" he shouted, knocking on the toy-shop door and ringing the bell.

"Here he is, Mr. Geppetto! Home at last!" I called.

Much to our disappointment, nobody came to the door.

"Maybe he's asleep!" said Pinocchio.

I peered into the window, which needed a good scrubbing, and saw that everything was dusty. Cobwebs covered Geppetto's workbench. I had a sinking feeling something was very wrong.

"He's not here," I told Pinocchio.

Pinocchio looked into the window with me.

"He . . . he's gone," he said in a shaky voice.

"Yeah—and so is Figaro," I noticed.

"And Cleo, too!" Pinocchio added. "Maybe something awful happened to them!"

I tried to make the little fellow feel better.

"Don't worry, son," I said. "They probably haven't gone far."

How completely wrong *that* turned out to be!

We sat on the front steps, trying to figure out what to do next.

Pinocchio sat with his head in his hands. I'd never seen him look so sad. Then, as if by magic, a piece of paper floated down from the sky and landed at my feet. I picked it up, put on my reading glasses, and examined it.

"Pinocchio!" I said excitedly. "It's a message about your father!"

"What's it say?" asked Pinocchio. "Where is he?"

"It says . . . he went looking for you," I said, reading on. "And . . . my, oh, my . . . he was swallowed by a whale!"

"Swallowed by a whale!" gasped Pinocchio.

"A whale named Monstro!" I continued. "But wait . . . your father's alive!"

"Alive?" asked Pinocchio. "Where?"

I was astonished at what the message said next. "He's still inside the whale!" I told Pinocchio. "At the bottom of the sea!"

"The bottom of the sea!" echoed Pinocchio.

I took off my glasses and tried to absorb what I had just read. Poor Geppetto! There was nothing anyone could do for him now!

Pinocchio walked off in a hurry.

"Hey, Pinoke!" I called. "Where are you going?"

"I'm going to find my father," announced Pinocchio, looking back over his shoulder at me. "I'm going to the bottom of the sea."

The bottom of the sea!

"Wait! Listen here!" I said, racing after him. "Are you crazy? Don't you realize—he's inside a whale!"

"I've got to go to him," said Pinocchio, starting to run.

"But this is Monstro," I said, running alongside of him. "I've heard of him—he's tough! He's a whale of a whale—he swallows whole ships!"

But Pinocchio was determined. And nothing I could say would stop him.

Once again, we headed to the sea. At the edge of a high cliff, Pinocchio tied a heavy rock to his donkey tail.

"This will weigh me down," he explained, "so I can walk on the bottom of the sea."

Pinocchio was ready to jump. "Good-bye, Jiminy," he said.

I just couldn't let the little guy go alone.

"I may be live bait down there," I said, grabbing on to his tail, "but I'm with you!"

And together we plunged the long way down into the water.

"Look out below!" I shouted, trying to sound brave, but I was really scared out of my wits!

The rock tied to Pinocchio's tail dragged us straight down to the ocean floor.

"Gee!" said Pinocchio, looking around. "What a big place!"

I let go of Pinocchio's tail and scouted around for something to weigh me down, too. I found a large stone and stuck it under my hat. Pretty soon I was upside down, so I put the rock down my pants instead. This seemed to do the trick.

We were an odd pair, with our weights attached, starting our search along the bottom of the sea.

"Fatherrrr!" called Pinocchio, his voice sounding bubbly and strange.

"Mr. Geppettoooo!" I called. This talking underwater wasn't going to be easy!

It was beautiful down there. The sun's rays lit twisting strands of seaweed, turning them gold. Some of the creatures looked more like brightly colored flowers than like sea animals. Striped fish darted in and out of coral caves and a herd of tiny sea horses followed close to us.

Pinocchio turned to a sea horse bobbling near his shoulder.

"Could you tell me where to find Monstro the whale?" he asked politely. The sea horse turned white, shivered with fright, and scurried off.

Over and over, the same thing happened. Every time we asked about Monstro, the poor sea creatures looked terrified and fled. It was clear that Monstro was really something monstrous!

But at that moment, Monstro awoke from his nap. He opened one huge eye just in time to see a school of tuna scurrying past. With one gigantic gulp, Monstro swallowed the entire school of tuna—and Pinocchio was sucked in right along with them!

*   *   *

Deep inside the whale's belly, Geppetto sat in his fishing boat. The whale was asleep and hadn't swallowed any fish for a long time. And if Monstro didn't eat something soon, Geppetto would starve.

"Not a bite for days," the old man said to Cleo and Figaro. "We can't hold out much longer."

Almost as if hearing Geppetto's plea, Monstro's mouth opened and a torrent of water rushed in.

"Look, Figaro!" cried Geppetto. "Tuna fish! Tons of them! We won't starve after all!" The tuna flapped wildly in the whale's belly and Geppetto's fishing boat rocked in the choppy water.

He threw his fishing line over the boat rail and pulled in the glistening fish, one after another. "That's enough for weeks," he cried to his pets.

Pinocchio swam frantically, tumbling around Monstro's belly with

the school of tuna. He grabbed the tail of a large fish just as Geppetto
yanked it out of the water.

"That one was *heavy*!" grunted Geppetto, tossing both the tuna
and Pinocchio over his shoulder.

"Father!" cried Pinocchio, landing on the deck in a pile of fish.

Geppetto continued to fish. "Don't bother me now, Pinocchio," he said. "P-Pinocchio!" Geppetto spun around. He couldn't believe his eyes!

"Pinocchio! My son!" he cried, picking up his little wooden boy and kissing him. "You're soaking wet!" he said. "You mustn't catch cold."

"Yes, Father," said Pinocchio, "but I came to save you. And to get you out of Monstro!"

"You shouldn't have come, Pinocchio, but I'm awfully glad to see you," said Geppetto. "Let me take your hat," he said as he took it from Pinocchio's head. Pinocchio's donkey ears popped out, and Geppetto jumped back.

"What's the matter, Father?" asked Pinocchio.

"Those ears!" Geppetto replied.

"Oh, these! Ha, ha—they're nothing," Pinocchio said, and laughed bashfully. "I've got a tail, too!"

"What's happened to you?" Geppetto asked, very surprised.

"Well," Pinocchio said with a sigh. "Well, you see, I . . ."

"Oh, never mind now," said Geppetto. "I have you back. Nothing else matters."

CHAPTER TEN

y the time I managed to make my way over to Monstro, it was all over! Monstro had shut his mouth and Pinocchio was inside!

I surprised myself with my bravery. I actually pounded on that whale with my umbrella and hit him on the mouth with my fist!

"Open up, blubbermouth!" I shouted. "I have to get in there!"

But it appeared that after his snack of several dozen tuna *and* Pinocchio, Monstro was taking another nap! An old bottle floated by, so I climbed aboard.

I was amazed when I saw curls of dark smoke seep from the corners of Monstro's mouth. How could a whale be on fire? I wondered. Then I figured it out. Pinocchio and Geppetto had lit a fire inside the whale, hoping he would sneeze them out!

Monstro became more and more uncomfortable. He snorted and coughed, turning the sea around me black with smoke.

I watched, feeling both wonder and fright as Monstro grunted and snorted and sniffed and heaved. There's nothing in the world to match a whale getting ready to sneeze! I knew this was my only chance to get in—and I did! As I bobbed around on the bottle, I heard Pinocchio's voice call out, "Hurry, Father!"

"We'll never get by those teeth," Geppetto answered in dismay.

I paddled furiously toward the voices. Then, with a fantastic *ahhhh-chooo!* Monstro sneezed, and out of his mouth flew the raft! Clinging to it for dear life were Geppetto, Pinocchio, Cleo, and Figaro.

"Hey!" I shouted. "Wait for me!"

The raft shot crazily through the water. Finally, it glided easily along the surface of the sea. Inside the bottle, I had safely reached the surface, too.

"We made it!" said Pinocchio. He scanned the horizon, looking for Monstro. "Where'd he go?" he asked worriedly. As if to answer

him, Monstro was suddenly upon them. Or rather, *under* them! The raft was balanced right on Monstro's back!

"Look out!" shouted Geppetto. "Here he is—hang on!"

The furious whale flipped the raft high in the air, spilling them all into the churning sea. Still inside the bottle, I frantically looked around and spotted Geppetto hanging on to a piece of the smashed raft. I could see the old man was slowly losing his grasp and sinking.

"Pinocchio," gasped Geppetto in a weak voice. "Swim for shore! Save yourself!"

"Hang on, Father," I heard Pinocchio yell. He struggled through

the water to his father. Just then, Monstro began another fierce attack. The last I remember of that terrible scene was Pinocchio pulling on Geppetto's shirt, trying hard to rescue him and swim to safety. Monstro charged close behind them with his enormous mouth open wide. I felt sure it was the end of my friends and me. Then, like a huge hand, a wave swept me up and threw me onto the dry shore.

I couldn't believe I'd made it alive! You can imagine my joy when, looking around me, I saw Geppetto. The old man was lying on his back and breathing hard, but he was safe. With the next wave, a

piece of wood washed ashore, carrying little Figaro and Cleo. It was a miracle—they had all survived. But where was Pinocchio?

I nervously looked around. "Pinocchio!" I called. But he didn't answer. I called again and again. Still no answer!

When I found him at last, my heart sank. Still as stone, the little wooden fellow lay facedown in a pool of water.

"Oh, Pinocchio," I cried, rushing to him. But he didn't move and I was sure he would never move again.

CHAPTER ELEVEN

1 don't remember much of the long walk home. We were worn out and our hearts were breaking. Geppetto carried Pinocchio's still body in one arm and Cleo's bowl in the other. Figaro and I trailed behind. We made a sad procession as we slowly headed for Geppetto's house.

Back in the shop, Geppetto placed Pinocchio gently on his bed and knelt next to it. "My brave little boy," he sobbed, burying his face in his hands. "You saved my life!"

I looked at Pinocchio, lying there with his donkey ears, and thought of all we'd been through together. A familiar voice interrupted my thoughts.

"Prove that you are brave, truthful, and unselfish," it said, "and someday, you will be a real boy!"

It was the Blue Fairy! I could hear her, but this time she did not appear in the room.

"Awake, Pinocchio, awake!" said the gentle voice.

As before, a shimmering light appeared, but this time it covered Pinocchio. And then, before my eyes, a wondrous thing happened. Pinocchio slowly opened his eyes and sat up! He looked at both sides of his hands. They were no longer hard and wooden; they were rosy and warm! He was a *real* boy!

"Father!" he cried. "Look at me! I'm alive!"

Geppetto feebly lifted his face from his hands.

"Pinocchio?" he said, blinking his teary eyes.

"I'm—I'm—*real*!" shouted the little boy. "Look at me!"

Geppetto picked up his son. "You're alive!" he cried with joy. "And you *are* a real boy!"

"Whee! Whoopee!" I shouted, throwing my hat high in the air.

"Ha, ha," laughed Geppetto, tears still in his eyes. "This calls for a celebration!"

As he always did when he was happy, Geppetto picked up his accordion and began to play a lively tune. Pinocchio and Figaro danced and pranced around the room. Splashing gaily in her bowl, Cleo also celebrated Pinocchio's return.

I looked at the happy sight and was reminded of my first night here. But now everything was so much better! I hopped over to the window and searched the starry sky to find the one star shining brighter than the rest.

"Thank you, Blue Fairy," I said, looking up at it. "He deserved to be a real boy!"

I noticed something twinkling on my coat. Pinned to my lapel was a shiny badge with two words engraved on it. Looking closely, I read, OFFICIAL CONSCIENCE! And not only that—the badge was solid gold! Well, I'll be! The Blue Fairy thought I'd done a good job!

Everything had turned out fine after all. But what an adventure we'd had! And it all started because a lonely old man believed in wishing on a star.